panda series

**PANDA books are for first readers
beginning to make their own way
through books.**

Strawberry Squirt

Written and illustrated by
PATRICE AGGS

THE O'BRIEN PRESS
DUBLIN

First published 2004 by The O'Brien Press Ltd,
12 Terenure Road East, Rathgar, Dublin 6, Ireland.
Tel: +353 1 4923333; Fax: +353 1 4922777
E-mail: books@obrien.ie
Website: www.obrien.ie.
Reprinted 2005, 2006.

ISBN-10: 0-86278-805-6
ISBN-13: 978-0-86278-805-6

British Library Cataloguing-in-Publication Data
Aggs, Patrice
Strawberry squirt. - (Panda series ; 27)
1.Games - Juvenile fiction
2.Rabbits - Juvenile fiction
3.Children's stories
I.Title 823.9'14[J]

The O'Brien Press receives
assistance from

3   4   5   6   7   8   9
06   07   08   09   10

Typesetting, layout, editing, design: The O'Brien Press Ltd
Printing: Cox & Wyman Ltd

Can YOU spot the panda
hidden in the story?

'It's a messy game, my boy.'
Banana Ears was telling
Short Legs about
Strawberry Squirt.

It was a game
the big rabbits played.
They played it **once** a year.
And today was the Big Day.

'Can I play?' asked Short Legs.
'I want to play!'

'Oh no,' said Banana Ears.
'Only the **big** rabbits are
allowed to play.
The Great Game of
Strawberry Squirt
is not for babies.'

'Show me how to play! Please,' begged Short Legs.

'Well, let's ask the others what they think,' said Banana Ears.

10

The other rabbits were
not happy.

'His legs are too short,'
one of them said.
'But I can run fast,'
said Short Legs.

'The rules will be
too tricky for him,'
said another rabbit.
'But what **are** the rules?'
asked Short Legs.

13

Rule Number One:

Two squashes are
the same as one squirt.
But four squirts
put you back at base.

Rule Number Two:

No jigging.
If anyone jigs, the umpire
has to wave his paw.

Rule Number Three:

Jogs are fine
but only one at a time.
Two jogs are the same as a jig.
You waggle your left ear
for two jogs
and your right leg
for four squirts.

'Got it?' asked Banana Ears.
'Um ... I think so ... '
said Short Legs.
But his head felt sore.

The biggest rabbit smiled.
'There's one other thing,'
he said. 'You must be
spotless when
the game begins.
One spot of strawberry juice ...
just one drop ... and you're out.'

'And you have a
big red spot
on you already,'
said another rabbit.

'Where?' asked Short Legs.
'On your back,'
said all the rabbits.

'I do?' asked Short Legs.
He turned this way
and that way.
But he couldn't see
his back.

'Sorry. You can't play,'
said the big rabbits.
Short Legs looked at
Banana Ears, but
Banana Ears said nothing.

Short Legs went away to think.
He kept trying to look
at his back.

'I wonder how that red spot
got there?' he said to himself.
'I must have stepped
on a strawberry.
Those big rabbits are right.
I can't play if I'm
already **squirted**.'

Then he had an idea.
There was a pond
at the end of the lane.
It was deep and clean.

'I'll just wash off the spot,'
he said. 'If I hurry
I can be back in time
to play the game.'

The pond at the end of the lane
was deep and clean.
But there were
lots of little bugs on top.
They looked like they were
playing a game.

'Don't jump in! Not yet!'
one of them yelled.
'Just wait. The game is
nearly over.'

Short Legs watched them.
They were zooming in and out.
They were skating very fast.
One of them was
just about to win.

And then he did!

'The **WINNER**!'

all the bugs shouted.
Short Legs cheered.

The bugs set up
the winners' stand.

27

There was a place for
the Gold Medal winner
and a place each for
the Silver and the Bronze.

Short Legs thought
there might be speeches.
'This will take forever,'
he said to himself.

'Excuse me,' said Short Legs.
'But could I just jump in the
pond for a minute?
I need to wash a red spot
off my back.'

All the bugs zoomed round
to look at Short Legs's back.
'What spot?' they all asked.
'The **big red one**,'
said Short Legs.

'There's **nothing** on your back,' said the bugs. 'Who told you there was a spot?'

Short Legs didn't say anything.

'Let's get on with the prizes,'
said the bugs.

The Bronze Medal bug
got up on his stand.

The Silver Medal
bug got up, too.

The Gold Medal bug
stood in the middle.

Then there were
lots of speeches.

Short Legs didn't listen.
'I need to think,' he said.

Short Legs sat down in
just the **wrong place**.

The Gold Medal bug
flew up in the air
and landed in just the
wrong place.

That bug did not get
his Gold Medal.

He got a ride back to
the strawberry patch instead.

'I'll show them!'
said Short Legs.
He was going to get
in that game.

The game was
just about to start.
The big rabbits were all ready.

Short Legs walked
right up to them.
'You were all just
fooling me,' he said.
'Let me play Strawberry Squirt.'

39

The other rabbits looked at
each other.
'Oh, okay,' they said.
'Just this once.'

'You have a **bug** on
your back,' one of them said.

'I'm not listening to you,'
said Short Legs.
'I know all about your tricks.'

The rabbits showed him
what to do:

You start at one end
and run down to
the other end
and try to squirt all the rabbits
with strawberry juice.

AND try to keep other rabbits
from squirting YOU.

'I'm ready,' said Short Legs.

Bang! They were off!

It was hard.

Short Legs tried to
remember the rules.

He tried to squirt and squash
and jog but not jig.

He wished his legs were longer.

Banana Ears was
in the next row.
'You're doing fine!'
Banana Ears shouted.
'Keep going!'

Short Legs kept going.
He *was* doing fine.

Then some big rabbits
got in the way.
They were fast and could
zoom in and out.
They tried to keep
Short Legs back.

They tried hard to squirt him.

'Hold on in there, Short Legs!'
Banana Ears yelled.
Short Legs tried to
hold on in there.

It was getting harder.
He was getting tired.

Two big rabbits were ready
to squirt him.

Short Legs did not know how
to get out of the way.

Suddenly, Short Legs heard
a voice in his ear.
'Jog to the right! **Now**!'
said the voice.

Short Legs jogged.

'Quick! Squirt and squash
to the left!'
the same voice said.

Short Legs squirted
and squashed.

'Now, zoom in and out!'
said the voice.

'Who are you?'
Short Legs asked.
'Who is that talking to me?'

'Just zoom,' the voice said.
'I know all about zooming
in and out. I just won a
Gold Medal for zooming.'
It was the Gold Medal bug!

'I **have** got a bug
on my back!'
shouted Short Legs.
'Just ZOOM!' said
the Gold Medal bug.

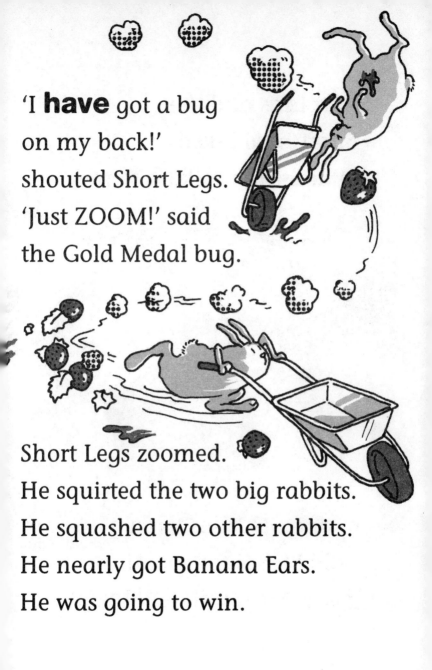

Short Legs zoomed.
He squirted the two big rabbits.
He squashed two other rabbits.
He nearly got Banana Ears.
He was going to win.

Short Legs and the
Gold Medal bug
could see the **finish line**.

One more squirt, and then —

HOORAY!!

'**You won**!'
shouted Banana Ears.

'**You won**!'

shouted the Gold Medal bug.

'**I won**!' shouted Short Legs.

The big rabbits set up
the winners' stand.
There was a place for the
Gold Medal winner
and a place each for the
Silver and the Bronze.

'I always knew you could do it!'
said Banana Ears.
'Oh you did, did you?'
said Short Legs.

'I told the others
you were good,'
said Banana Ears.
'I didn't hear you say
anything,' said Short Legs.

'Never mind all that,'
said Banana Ears.
'The fact is, you've won.
There will be speeches.
Get up on that winners' stand,
my boy.'

'Not yet,' said Short Legs.
'I have another winners' stand
to get back to.'

Short Legs and the
Gold Medal bug went back
to the pond at the end
of the lane.
Banana Ears ran after them.

All the bugs cheered
when they got there.

'Hooray! Our Gold Medal
winner!' they shouted.
'He made **me** a
Gold Medal winner, too!'
said Short Legs.

Everyone cheered again.

There were lots of speeches.
This time, Short Legs listened.
When it was all over,
the bugs asked Short Legs
to jump in the pond for a party.

'No, no,' said Banana Ears.
'Maybe later. Right now,
I need the Gold Medal rabbit.
I need to get him ready
for Raspberry Rush.'

'Raspberry Rush?'
asked Short Legs.
'What's that?'

'It's a messy game, my boy ...'
said Banana Ears.